D0833120

MOON MISSION

ISBN# 1-930710-46-1
Copyright ©2000 Veritas Press

Veritas Press
1250 Belle Meade Drive
Lancaster, PA 17601

First edition

MOON MISSION

Words: Tom Garfield

Pictures: NASA

This story is dedicated to
Carolyn, Seth, Kajsa and **Kathryn;**
my own little **space cadets.**

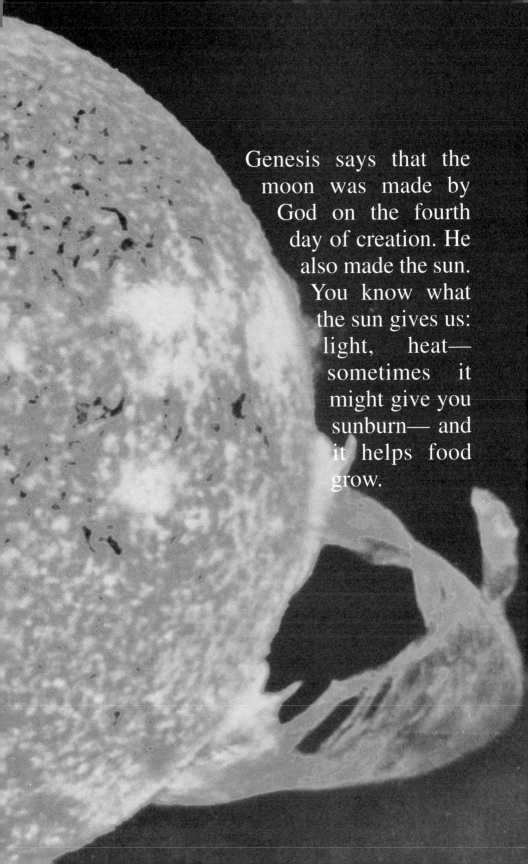

Genesis says that the moon was made by God on the fourth day of creation. He also made the sun. You know what the sun gives us: light, heat— sometimes it might give you sunburn— and it helps food grow.

Without the sun there would soon be much starvation on the earth. The sun makes its own light like a fire. Yet how can the moon have the light that we see during the night?

The moon's light is a reflection of the sun's light. If you shine a light on a mirror, the light bouces back at you. This is a reflection. That is how the moon shines at night. You could almost say the moon is God's big night light for all the nations.

For generations men have said, "We want to go to the moon." However, the moon is about 240,000 miles away. That is as far as going all the way around the world sixty

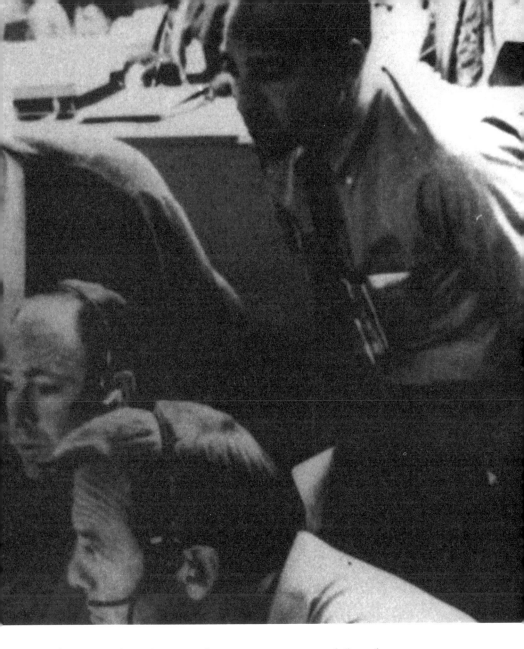

times. A trip to the moon would take a great imagination and a lot of innovation. The moon is out in space where there is no air to breathe.

So what kind of transportation would you need to get to the moon? Do you know? Yes, a rocket! The invention of big rockets did not take place until about fifty years ago. The first rockets did not always work right. Sometimes they would crash and make a big explosion!

Animals also took part in research before man went into space. They were given tests to help make space travel safe for men.

In 1961 the President of the United States, John F. Kennedy, told our nation that we were going to have a mission to put a man on the moon. It was his vision that we would try to do that in less than nine years.

That same year an American with great determination went up into space for the first

time. His name was Alan Shepard.

Our spacemen are "astronauts." That is their job or occupation. Astronauts must meet special qualifications. They need lots of education and training. They must be strong and smart. They also must be brave. They must be calm under lots of tension.

The first astronauts went into space in a small space capsule that was shot up into space on top of a tall, powerful rocket. There was a separation by the rocket section when it ran out of fuel, but the capsule went on.

Some astronauts were able to get out

of the capsule for a portion of the time while they were in space. They could float like a balloon on a string because there is no gravity in space.

However there were some problems, too. Three of our astronauts were lost in an explosion when they were in the space capsule still on the ground. That made some men have hesitation about the moon mission. Soon the corrections were made, and they went on bravely.

Finally, on July 16, 1969, three astronauts were set to go on the mission to the moon. The mission was given the name "Apollo 11." The men were in the big space capsule on top of the very tall rocket.

Soon they heard... "5,4,3,2,1, Ignition! Lift-off!" The rocket made a great roar! They were off to the moon to land on it! The duration of the flight was almost four days to get there.

They went very fast, but they did not feel much motion. When they got close to the moon, the space capsule had a division into two big sections. One section had to stay high above the moon with one astronaut, Michael Collins, to drive it.

The other section would land on the moon with the other two astronauts in it. This would take much coordination. The landing section was the Lunar (Latin translation for "moon") Module. It had the name "Eagle".

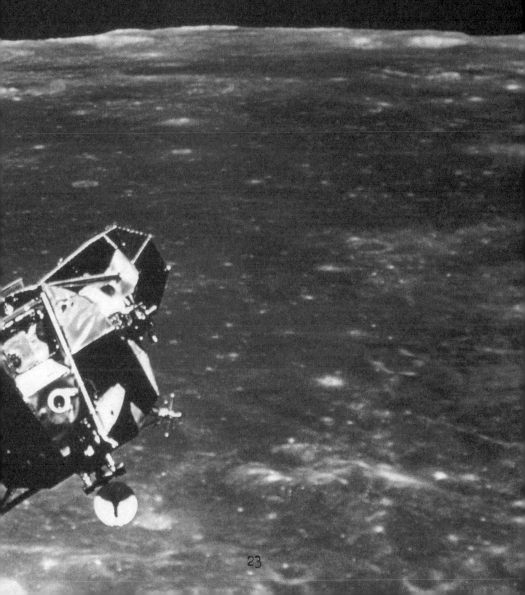

On July 20, 1969, the Eagle got closer and closer to the moon. Millions of people from many nations were watching it on television. Suddenly the ground of the moon could be seen and the commander of the Eagle,

Neil Armstrong, said with great expression that the Eagle is on the moon! Neil Armstrong had his space gear on and he went out of the door of the Eagle.

He went down a short ladder to step onto the dusty ground of the moon. With some interruptions, millions of people saw him and heard him say that he was taking "one small step for man, one giant leap for mankind."

With God's protection, men had made it to the moon! The ground of the moon was a firm foundation, but it had no plants, no water, and there was no air. The other astronaut, Edwin Aldrin, came out to walk on the moon, too.

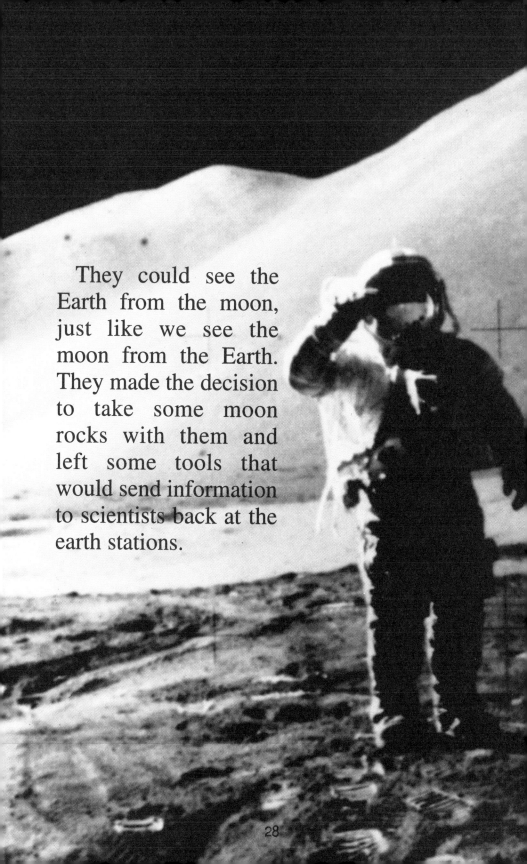

They could see the
Earth from the moon,
just like we see the
moon from the Earth.
They made the decision
to take some moon
rocks with them and
left some tools that
would send information
to scientists back at the
earth stations.

There was not much traction and gravity, so the men had to bounce, not walk, when they were on the moon. They put up an American flag on a pole.

Then it was time to go back. The Eagle shot off the moon and made a connection with the other section of the capsule in space. When the astronauts got back to Earth there was a great celebration!

So the next time you look up at the moon, remember that God let men walk there.

About the Photography:

Cover: Edwin Aldrin, Lunar Module Pilot (Neil Armstrong is in the reflection).

Page 6: The Sun experiencing the largest solar flare ever recrded by NASA's Skylab 4 (367,000 miles long).

Page 8:Earth View (Starburst Sunrise)

Page 10:Space Center, Houston. A group of astronauts keep track of the troubled Apollo 13.

Page 12: Apollo 11 rises past the launch tower at pad 39A, 9:32 a.m. EDT, July 16, 1969.

Page 14: John F. Kennedy and Astronaut John H. Glenn look into the porthole of the *Mercury*.

Page 16: Mercury Little Joe launch at Wallops Island, Virginia.

Page 18: Exterior of the Apollo/saturn 204 spacecraft, following a fire which killed the 204 prime crew members.

Page 22: Apollo II lunar module ascent.

Page 24:Mission Control Center, Manned Spacecraft Center, Houston, Texas.

Page 26: Edwin Aldrin deploying Passive Seismic Experiments Package.

Page 28:David Scott saluting the U.S. flag near the mountain called Hadley Delta.

Page 30: Apollo 17 Pacific Recovery Area.